ISLAND MAGIC

Illustrated by
Daniel San Souçi

Atheneum Books for Young Readers

ISLAND
MAGIC

by Martha Bennett Stiles

Atheneum Books for Young Readers
An imprint of Simon & Schuster Children's Publishing Division
1230 Avenue of the Americas
New York, New York 10020

Book design by Nina Barnett
The text of this book is set in Janson Text.
The illustrations are rendered in watercolors.
Printed in Hong Kong
10 9 8 7 6 5 4 3 2 1
Library of Congress Cataloging-in-Publication Data
Stiles, Martha Bennett.
Island magic / by Martha Bennett Stiles; illustrated by Daniel San Souçi.—1st ed.
p.   cm.
Summary: When Grandad comes to live with David and his family on their island, he and David
enjoy sharing the wonders of the natural world.
ISBN 0-689-80588-8
[1. Nature—Fiction. 2. Islands—Fiction. 3. Grandfathers—Fiction.] I. San Souçi, Daniel, ill. II. Title.
PZ7.S8557Is   1998   [E]—dc20   96-21181

For Greg and Kevin Wells, Burgin and Will Dossett,
and Ben and Ted Murray
—M. B. S.

For Jimmy and Julianna Muzzini
—D. S. S.

Last February my grandfather sold his dairy farm and came
to live with me and my parents. We live on a big island in the
Detroit River.

I was glad when I heard that Grandad was coming. My parents and I had visited his farm every year. Grandad and I always walked to the barn together, and he told me interesting things.

The first morning Grandad was here, I got up before the herons left their roost. Grandad was already dressed in his winter milking clothes, sitting in a rocking chair on our front porch.

Ships go by our house carrying freight: limestone and iron ore, grain and coal. Grandad was watching a slow fat black freighter.

"Pancakes for breakfast!" I told him.

"Tell your mother I'm not hungry this morning, thank you, David," Grandad said.

Mom and Dad looked worried. "He misses his black cows," Mom said. "He knew every one by name. His favorite was I O *U*."

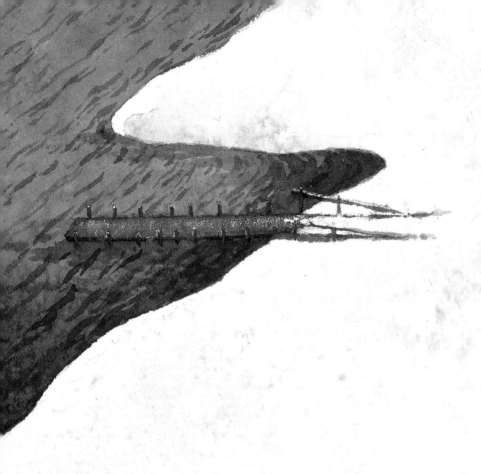

I was worried too. I went back out on the cold porch. Grandad was rocking. His breath made thin fog.

"All the ships that go by our island have names, printed on their sides," I told Grandad. The trouble is, we never see the same ship two days running.

"Our *island* has a name," I tried again. "It's Grosse Ile. Grosse Ile is French for Big Island."

Grandad patted my head and went on rocking.

I remembered how before Grandad sold his cows, he fed them before breakfast every day.

Reeds grow where our yard meets the water. Wild geese shelter there all winter. I asked Grandad to come with me, and I showed him how I feed them corn.

"I fed my cows corn too," Grandad reminded me.

Watching the geese gobble corn made Grandad and me hungry. We went in to breakfast together.

Mom makes the best pancakes in Michigan except for Dad's, and I ate six.

Granddad ate two and said they were good. I wanted to ask him if he was glad he'd come to our island, but I was afraid he might say no. I tried to think what else I could show him.

"We could name our geese," I said hopefully.

All the rest of the winter, Grandad and I fed the geese together. We took turns choosing names for them. I named one Fussy Gussie and one Dirty Gertie. Grandad named one Sir Gansalot and one Sir Lunchalot. The names we gave them made Grandad smile, but he never said he was glad he'd come to our island, and all February I was afraid to ask.

Behind our house we have an elderberry bush and four apple trees. In spring, I showed Grandad the rosebreasted grosbeak's nest in our bush.

"Grosbeak is French for big beak," I told Grandad.

I showed Grandad the robin's nest in our Jonathan apple tree.

"Rosebreasted grosbeaks," Grandad told me, "are robins that took singing lessons."

I wanted Grandad to tell me more things. I wanted him to stop missing his cows. I wanted him to like living on my island as much as I do.

The birds sang in our apple trees all summer. Still Grandad never said he was glad he'd come, and all summer I was still afraid to ask.

One autumn morning I could hear lots of ship horns, but I couldn't see one ship. Fog covered the river.

Grandad and I fed the geese. A patch of fog moved slowly from the edge of the lake across our yard.

"It drifts like a cow eating grass," I told Grandad.

The fog felt damp on our hands.

"Like a cow's breath," Grandad said.

We stood awhile and listened to the ships' foghorns bellowing. "Like bulls calling to their cows," Grandad said.

The fog in our yard split into three pieces, one big and two little. The big one browsed up the yard toward Grandad and me. The two little ones followed.

"Like a cow with twins," I said, "one for you, and one for me."

Grandad squeezed my hand, and I squeezed back.

"Mom says fogs come when our island starts getting cooler than our river," I said. "We have fogs every fall."

"I like living here where you can tell me things," Grandad told me. He put his arm around my shoulder and we went in to breakfast together.

I ate seven pancakes and Grandad ate five.